T3-BAN-126

OUT OF THIS WORLD

THE UNIVERSE

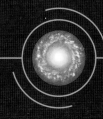

KELLY DOUDNA

Consulting Editor, Diane Craig, M.A./Reading Specialist

Super Sandcastle

An Imprint of Abdo Publishing
abdopublishing.com

ABDOPUBLISHING.COM

Published by Abdo Publishing, a division of ABDO, PO Box 398166, Minneapolis, Minnesota 55439. Copyright © 2016 by Abdo Consulting Group, Inc. International copyrights reserved in all countries. No part of this book may be reproduced in any form without written permission from the publisher. Super SandCastle™ is a trademark and logo of Abdo Publishing.

Printed in the United States of America, North Mankato, Minnesota
062015
092015

THIS BOOK CONTAINS RECYCLED MATERIALS

Editor: Liz Salzmann
Content Developer: Nancy Tuminelly
Cover and Interior Design and Production: Mighty Media, Inc.
Photo Credits: NASA, Shutterstock

Library of Congress Cataloging-in-Publication Data
Doudna, Kelly, 1963- author.
  The universe / Kelly Doudna ; consulting editor, Diane Craig, M.A./Reading Specialist.
    pages cm. -- (Out of this world)
  Audience: K to grade 4
  ISBN 978-1-62403-747-4
1. Cosmology--Juvenile literature. 2. Galaxies--Juvenile literature. 3. Universe--Juvenile literature. I. Title.
  QB857.3.D68 2016
  523.1--dc23
                          2015002062

Super SandCastle™ books are created by a team of professional educators, reading specialists, and content developers around five essential components—phonemic awareness, phonics, vocabulary, text comprehension, and fluency—to assist young readers as they develop reading skills and strategies and increase their general knowledge. All books are written, reviewed, and leveled for guided reading, early reading intervention, and Accelerated Reader™ programs for use in shared, guided, and independent reading and writing activities to support a balanced approach to literacy instruction.

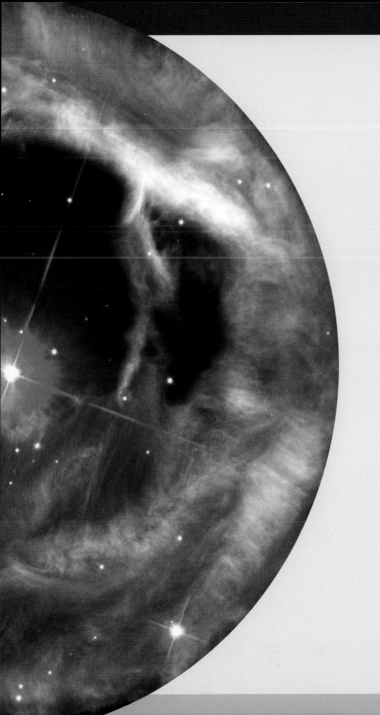

CONTENTS

THE UNIVERSE

NOW YOU SEE IT

We see many things in the universe. It has planets, stars, and galaxies. But they are a small part of the universe.

NOW YOU DON'T

The universe has many things we can't see. It is full of **dark matter** and **dark energy**.

THE UNIVERSE IS EVERYTHING IN SPACE.

IN THE DARK

For each thing we can see, there are 19 we can't see!

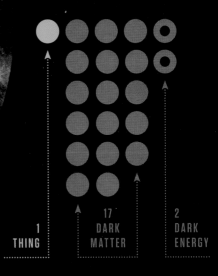

1
THING

17
DARK
MATTER

2
DARK
ENERGY

THE BIG BANG

The universe was small. It was smaller than the head of a pin. Then everything exploded!

The explosion is called the Big Bang. Suddenly the universe was bigger than a galaxy. It took one second.

THE UNIVERSE BEGAN WITH THE BIG BANG.

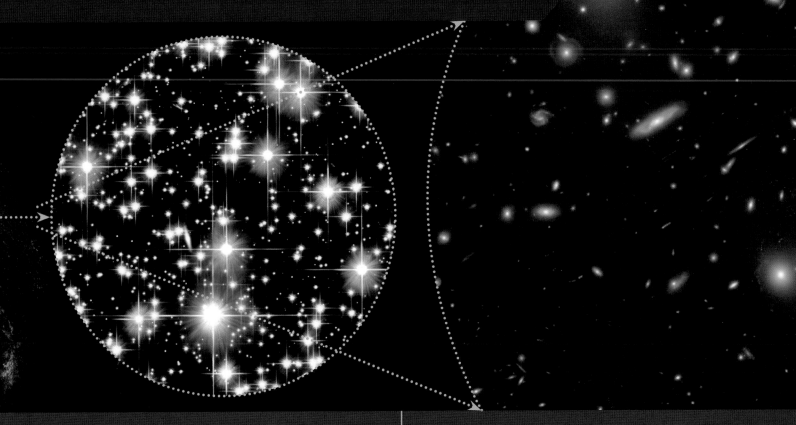

The universe grew. Stars formed 100 million years after the Big Bang.

The universe is almost 14 **billion** years old. It has always been growing. It is still growing!

THE SHAPE OF THE UNIVERSE

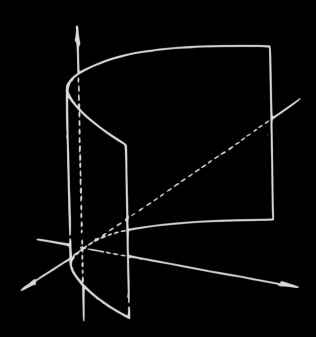

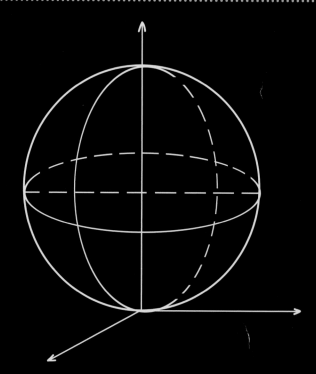

FLAT

A flat universe would look flat.

SPHERICAL

A spherical universe would be shaped like a ball.

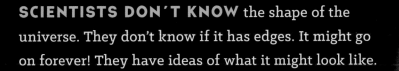

SCIENTISTS DON'T KNOW the shape of the universe. They don't know if it has edges. It might go on forever! They have ideas of what it might look like.

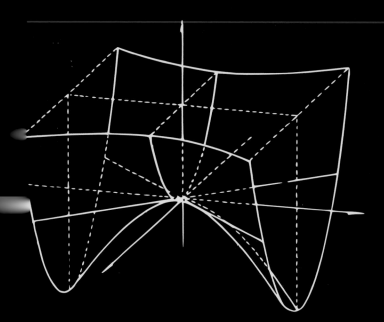

HYPERBOLIC

A hyperbolic universe would be shaped like a horse saddle.

MULTIVERSE

Multi- means *many*. There could be many universes.

THE UNIVERSE

SOLAR SYSTEM

Earth is part of the solar system. The sun is the center of the solar system. Everything in the solar system circles around the sun.

STARS

There are more stars than grains of sand on Earth.

NEBULA

A cloud of dust and gas is called a nebula.

WE CAN SEE

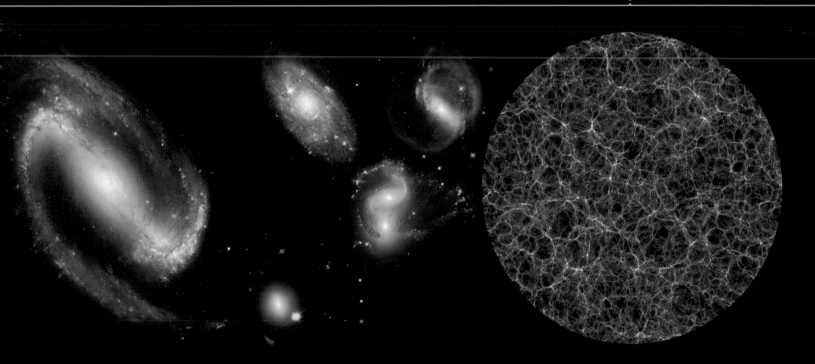

GALAXY

A group of stars is
a galaxy. A galaxy
has **billions** of stars.

CLUSTER

Many galaxies make a group. Many
galaxy groups make a cluster. Many
galaxy clusters make a supercluster.

THE COSMIC WEB

Galaxy clusters group together.
They make strings and walls.
This is called the cosmic web.

GALAXIES

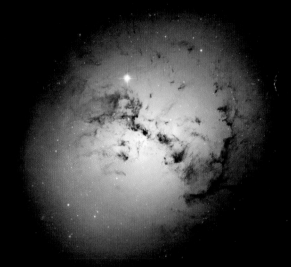

GLOBULAR CLUSTERS AND DWARF GALAXIES

These are small galaxies. A dwarf galaxy has a few million stars.

ELLIPTICAL GALAXIES

Elliptical galaxies look rounded. Some are shaped like a ball. Others are shaped like a jelly bean.

GALAXY FACT

Newer stars are on the edge of a galaxy. Old stars are near the middle of a galaxy.

THERE ARE A LOT of galaxies. They come in many shapes. They can be different sizes too!

SPIRAL GALAXIES

A spiral galaxy has arms. It looks like a big swirl.

IRREGULAR GALAXIES

An irregular galaxy has a different shape. It is not elliptical or spiral.

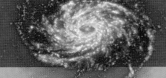

THE MILKY WAY

Earth is in the Milky Way galaxy. The Milky Way is a spiral galaxy.

STARS

THE BEGINNING

A nebula is made of dust and gas. Sometimes the dust and gas sticks together. This creates a new star.

EARLY LIFE

A star burns gas. It makes the star shine. Smaller stars live longer. Larger stars have a shorter life.

THE SUN

Earth's sun is an average star. It is more than four **billion** years old. It is halfway through its life.

A star can live for **trillions** of years. Then it dies.

LATER LIFE

A star runs out of gases to burn. It cools down. As the star cools, it gets bigger. It looks reddish. An average star becomes a red giant. A **massive** star becomes a red supergiant.

THAT'S BIG!

The sun will become a red giant. It will be big enough to touch Earth!

THE END OF STARS

WHITE DWARF

NEBULA

RED GIANTS

An average star becomes a red giant. A red giant loses its outer shell of gas. This becomes a nebula. What is left in the middle is a white dwarf. Our sun will become a white dwarf.

STARS END DIFFERENTLY. THE SIZE OF A STAR AFFECTS HOW IT WILL END.

SUPERNOVA!

SUPERGIANT SUPERNOVA

A **massive** star goes out with a bang! It becomes a red supergiant. Then the red supergiant **collapses** fast. This makes the star explode. The explosion is called a supernova.

NEUTRON STAR

The center of the star collapses. It becomes a neutron star. Neutron stars are tiny.

BLACK HOLE

Sometimes the center will collapse more. It becomes a black hole.

NEBULAE

A **NEBULA** is a cloud. It is made of dust and gas. Nebulae are made in different ways.

IN THE MIDDLE

Gas and dust sit in the space between stars. The gas and dust form a nebula.

STAR COLLAPSE

When a red giant **collapses** it can make a nebula. It is not very bright.

LEFTOVER SUPERNOVA

A supernova leaves behind dust and gas. It becomes a nebula. New stars are made from this kind of nebula.

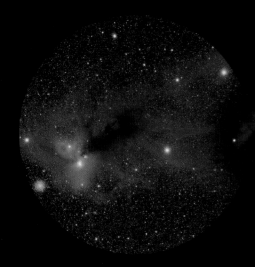

INTERSTELLAR MEDIUM

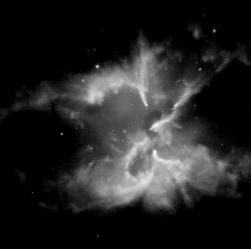

PLANETARY NEBULA

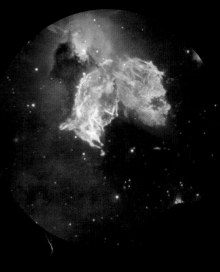

SUPERNOVA REMNANT

18

BLACK HOLES

RED GIANT ··············▶

BLACK HOLE

BLACK HOLE FACT
Many galaxies have a black hole at their centers.

A **massive** star **collapses**. All of the **matter** is pushed into a tiny space. Gravity becomes strong there. Nothing can escape its pull. It is a black hole.

SYSTEMS

STAR SYSTEM

Sometimes two or more stars orbit each other. This is a star system. A two-star system is called a **BINARY STAR**. A three-star system is called a **TRIPLE STAR**.

SPACE OBJECTS CAN KEEP CIRCLING EACH OTHER.
A GROUP OF THESE IS A SYSTEM.

PLANETARY SYSTEM

Sometimes objects orbit a star.
This is a planetary system. Earth's
solar system is a planetary system.
Planets orbit the sun.

GOING ROGUE

CRASHING GALAXIES

ROGUE PLANETS

A rogue planet does not circle a star. It circles the center of a galaxy.

ROGUE STARS

A rogue star is not part of a galaxy. Galaxies crash into each other. Stars get thrown off course. They become rogue stars.

STILL LEARNING

The universe has many **secrets**. Scientists work to uncover them. They discover new things every day!

THE UNIVERSE QUIZ

1. The universe has things we can't see. *True or false?*

2. What is the shape of the Milky Way galaxy?

3. What is a two-star system called?

THINK ABOUT IT!

What new things do you think will be discovered about the universe?

Answers 1. True 2. Spiral 3. Binary star

GLOSSARY

billion – a very large number. One billion is also written 1,000,000,000.

collapse – to give way or fold in on itself.

dark energy – energy in the universe. It cannot be measured.

dark matter – the "stuff" scientists think one-quarter of the universe is made up of. It is not visible to the eye.

massive – large and heavy.

matter – something that has weight and takes up space.

trillion – a very large number. One trillion is also written 1,000,000,000,000.

31901064717608